FREDDIE AS F.R.O.7.

CARTOON BOOK 2

Freddie Goes to London

Jon Acevski and David Ashton

WARNER BOOKS

Freddie Goes to London
A Warner Book

First published in Great Britain in 1992 by Warner Books

Copyright © Hollywood Road Film Productions Limited 1992

The moral right of the authors has been asserted.

Design by Between The Lines
Illustrated by HRFP Artists
Adaptation by Belinda Hollyer

A CIP catalogue record for this book is available from the British Library.

ISBN 0 356 20115 5

Printed by Graphicom SRL, Italy

Warner Books
A Division of Little, Brown and Company (UK) Limited
165 Great Dover Street
London SE1 4YA

The Freddie Library

Have you read all the Freddie books? These are the titles:

FREDDIE AS FR07
PRINCE FREDERIC   THE ISLE OF WORMS
FREDDIE GOES TO LONDON   FREDDIE SAVES THE DAY

All Freddie books are available at your bookshop or newsagent, or can be ordered from:
Little, Brown and Company (UK) Limited, PO Box 11, Falmouth, Cornwall TR10 9EN.
Alternatively you may fax your order to the above address on: 0326 376423.

Payments can be made as follows: cheque, postal order (payable to Little, Brown and Company)
or credit card, Visa/Access, with card number and expiry date. Do not send cash or currency.
UK customers and BFPO allow £1.00 for postage and packing for the first book, plus 50p for the
second book, plus 30p for each additional book up to a maximum charge of £3.00 (7 books plus).
Overseas customers including Ireland, allow £2.00 for the first book
plus £1.00 for the second book plus 50p for each additional book.

Many years passed, and Freddie had left being a frog-prince far behind him. He was a famous secret agent, based in Paris. Freddie used only his secret, magic powers and his cleverness to fight crime

He never used weapons, and his only help came from Nicole, his custom-made Frogmobile with a mind of her own!

Freddie's fame spread throughout the world. So when MI5, the British Secret Service, were baffled by a series of strange crimes, they decided to contact him.
"Yes, yes," Freddie agreed.
"I'll come to London at once!"

For, in London, a
frightening thing
was happening.

One by one, London's famous monuments were disappearing! The first thing to go was Nelson's Column, from its home in Trafalgar Square. And it happened right in front of a group of tourists and their guide!

"Now, ladies and gentlemen," said the guide, "on the left you'll see one of England's most famous and best-loved monuments . . . ."

"Nelson's Column . . ."
But the words stuck in
the guide's throat, as
everyone looked up to
see that the column had
disappeared.

"I don't see nothing," said one
young tourist.
   "Are you *sure* this is Trafalgar
Square?" asked another.

6

And not far away, above the River Thames, two old ravens admired the view as they flew back to their home at the Tower of London.

They agreed there was nothing nicer than to fly around at lunchtime – above the bridges, across to the Houses of Parliament . . .

. . . along to St Paul's Cathedral, and then back down past London Bridge, to the Tower.

But at the Tower of London, something very strange happened.

Without any warning, the Tower disappeared, leaving the other ravens with nowhere to roost.

"Yes, what I always say is
. . . *oh h*
         e
           l
             p!"
And the two old ravens
crashed to the ground, as
they tried to land on top
of where the Tower
should have been!

Two young punk ravens helped them up.
　"Where's the Tower gone?" asked the old lady raven. "Or am I dreaming?"

"I hope they haven't sold it," grumbled the old man raven in a gloomy voice.
　"Well, what I always say," said his friend, "is . . . *oh help!*" And she burst into tears.

That afternoon the Queen arrived in Pall Mall in her coach. A TV newscaster spoke to the cameras. "Home at last," he said. "As Her Majesty returns after her six-week tour abroad, she must be reflecting that there's no place like home . . ."

". . . and although Buckingham Palace is a palace to the rest of us, to Her Majesty it is simply her home . . ."

The newscaster stopped dead. A strange beam of light had descended from the sky, and Buckingham Palace tilted, then lifted into the air.

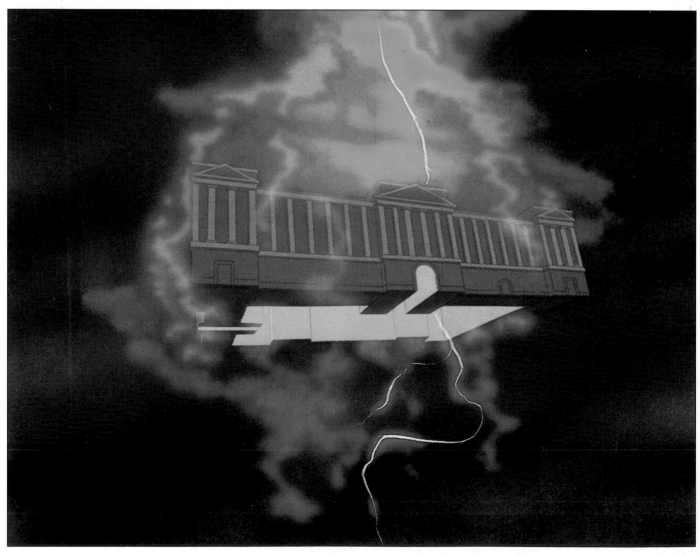

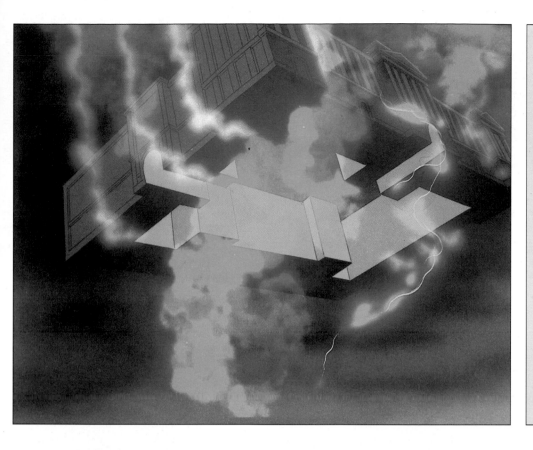

Up the Palace rose on the beam of light, and finally disappeared completely into the clouds.

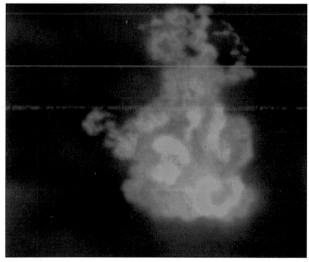

The crowd was amazed. Pandemonium broke out, as everyone tried to make sense of what they'd seen.

The Queen's coachman
leaned down to the
window.
"Erm . . . Your
Majesty, I don't know
how to tell you, but . . .
Buckingham Palace
seems to have gone."

"Gone? Gone? *Where* has it
gone?" replied the Queen.
"I dunno," answered the
coachman. "I suppose the
aliens must have got it . . . "

At MI5 that evening, the Brigadier, who was in charge of locating the missing monuments, was on the telephone to the Prime Minister.

"Yes, I realise that Her Majesty must have been fairly upset that Buckingham Palace wasn't quite . . . all there. Oh yes, *very* upset, very upset indeed. . ."

"Yes, I know that Britain's best-loved historic buildings are disappearing . . . What am I going to do about it? Erm . . . I have a plan in the pipeline, a jolly good plan!"

The Brigadier laughed nervously. "Don't worry, Prime Minister, we'll be back to normal in no time."

As the Prime Minister slammed down the phone, the Brigadier turned to his staff. "Come on you fools, get me out of this mess!"

The Brigadier moaned softly to himself. "This couldn't have come at a worse time. I've just lost some of my best undercover agents – 003 in China, 005 in Russia, and 007 in Hollywood . . ."

Just then the two young punk ravens flew into the room. "Hey, Daddio," they mocked, "the Tower of London's gone! Wotcha gonna do about it, huh?"

The Brigadier and his staff were baffled – except for Trilby.

"I wonder what's going to be next?" Trilby asked innocently, as he secretly chose two more pegs from his box. The pegs were for Stonehenge and St Paul's Cathedral.

From the radio a voice said, "Stonehenge is missing! Stonehenge is missing! And St Paul's is missing! St Paul's is missing!"

As everyone else groaned in dismay, Trilby gave a small smile. Then he pressed his pegs into place.

"I thought you said you had a plan, Sir?" Trilby reminded the Brigadier.

21

"I do have a plan," replied the Brigadier. "I've asked the French Secret Service to send over their top man."

"He's the best in the world," continued the Brigadier, cheering up. "He's the one who defeated the Blue Brigade, and stopped the Hanoi Hijack single-handed. He's none other than . . .

. . . the famous FR07!"

"A Frenchman?" sneered Trilby. "Surely we don't need the help of a garlic eater?"

"We need all the help we can get!" answered the Brigadier angrily.

Just then, the door opened. "FR07 has arrived, Sir, in an *incredible* automobile!"

"Show him in," said the Brigadier.

"Sir . . . just to warn you," added the doorman, "he's . . . a frog!"

"That's no way to talk about our loyal French allies!" snapped the Brigadier.

"No, Sir, what I mean is – he's **green**!"

"Nonsense!" replied the Brigadier. "He's their most experienced man! Show him in at once!"

23

"Now come on men," continued the Brigadier. "Straighten up! Let's show FR07 what the British Secret Service is made of!"

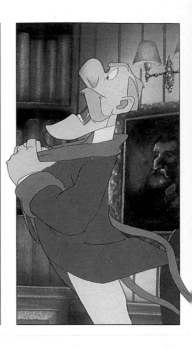

Freddie's eyes twinkled at everyone's stunned reaction.

"But . . . you're a frog!" stuttered the Brigadier, forgetting his manners. Trilby laughed rudely, and the Brigadier glared at him.

"I understand you have a slight problem," said Freddie. "Something about disappearing buildings . . . ?"

"Oh, so you've been briefed about it, have you?" asked the Brigadier, recovering himself.

"But of course," answered Freddie.

"We must get our buildings back, FR07," said the Brigadier. "Come on. Let me show you around while we talk."

"I can guarantee you the backing of all our facilities," promised the Brigadier. "Scientific gadgets, for instance: you name 'em, we've got 'em!"

"Can we de-activate the flying bug, please?" said the Brigadier to the woman. Then he introduced her to Freddie.

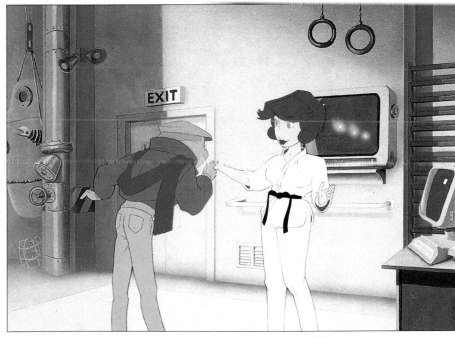

"This is Daphne Fortescue-Fortescue, one of our best boffins. Call her Daffers."

"I'm delighted to meet you, Daffers," replied Freddie, "but I'm afraid I don't have any use for gadgets."

"Then what about weapons?" asked the Brigadier, as they walked into the weapons section.

"This is Scotty McGunn, head of the weapons section. He can get you anything . . .

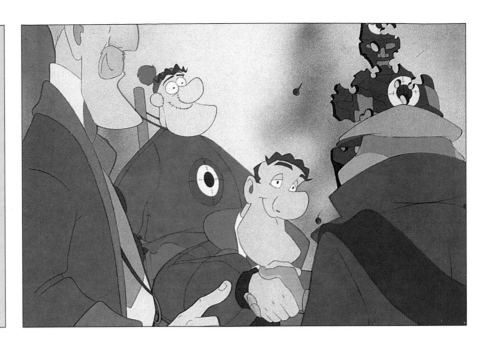

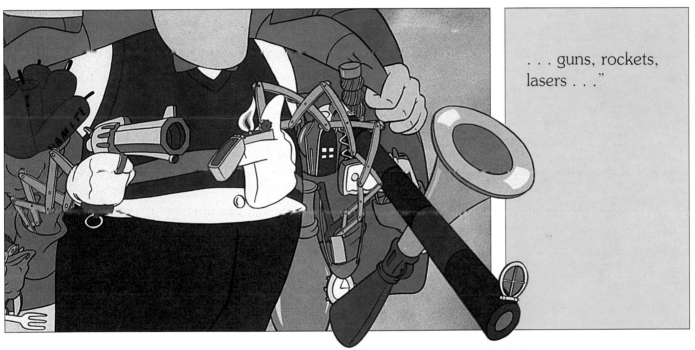

. . . guns, rockets, lasers . . ."

"The only weapons I ever use are my thoughts," said Freddie politely. "The powers of the mind will always overcome violence."

Just then there was a
news flash on the
video screen.
"Canterbury Cathedral
has disappeared!"

As the Brigadier answered his
telephone, he turned to Freddie.
"Will you take the job?" he asked.
   Freddie smiled. "How can I
refuse?" he replied.

"You can have Daffers
and Scotty to help you!"
offered the Brigadier.
   "Well," replied
Freddie, "I usually work
alone – but this time I'll
make an exception."
   "We won't let you
down," promised Scotty.

"Well off you go then, and the best of luck!" cried the Brigadier. "Oh, hello Prime Minister . . ."

"Yes, I heard that the Cathedral has gone – bad show, what? No, don't worry, I have the situation under control . . ."

"Poor old Brigadier G," murmured Daffers. "What a job!"

"Where do we make a start, Freddie?" asked Scotty.

"Yes," added Trilby mockingly, "where *are* you going to start?"

"Well," answered Freddie, "I've always wanted to go to the English races, so why not start at Ascot?"

"What a quaint idea," sneered Trilby. He looked at his watch. "You must *excuse* me, I have a date."

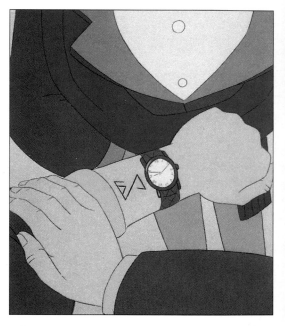

"And I have to catch a master criminal," replied Freddie, "so *excuse me*." He turned to Daffers and Scotty. "Come on, *mes amis!*"

Dressed in their smart clothes, Freddie, Daffers and Scotty set off for Ascot in the Frogmobile.

Everything went well until they got stuck in a traffic jam, and Nicole grew impatient. "Now, behave yourself, Nicole," warned Freddie.

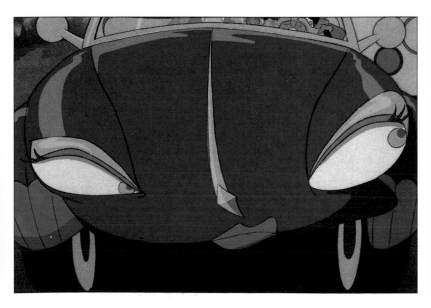

But Nicole took no notice. She gently hopped up on to the roof of the car in front – and off she went, jumping from car to car!

Unfortunately, one car had an open top . . . but Nicole didn't wait for Freddie to apologise!

It didn't take long to get to the races. Freddie and Daffers looked very smart, but Scotty was uncomfortable in his outfit. The three companions walked slowly through the Ascot crowds.

"Freddie, do you mind telling me what *we're* doing here?" asked Scotty at last.

"We must be up against a massive organisation, with spies all over the country," explained Freddie.

"And the only way to smoke spies out of the woodpile is to make yourself a sitting duck!"

"Aye," agreed Scotty gloomily, pulling unsuccessfully at his hat. "I'm certainly doing that part well!"

"So, Daffers," asked Freddie, "what horse do you want to bet on in the next race?"

"I thought I'd put my money on Number Seven," replied Daffers.

"A good choice," said Freddie.

"It's a French horse – I'll do the same!" said Scotty.

"OK," said Freddie loudly for the benefit of any spies. "I'll put the bets on now. Wait here – I shan't be long."

"Twenty to one is a very good price. I'll bet on Number Seven – I can't lose!"

"We have a message for you, FR07," hissed the leader of the spies. "And the message is – death!"

"Well," murmured Freddie, "you had better give me the message!"

But as the spies tried to grab his hand, Freddie knocked all four of them to the ground.

Then, with a super-powerful leap, Freddie soared to the top of the terrace. The spies couldn't *see* him. "He's escaped!" they gasped, looking wildly around.

"We must report this," said the leader in despair, reaching for his walkie-talkie.

Far above them, Freddie leaned over the edge of the terrace. He could hear every word. "Leader to El Supremo, leader to El Supremo," said the spy into his walkie-talkie.

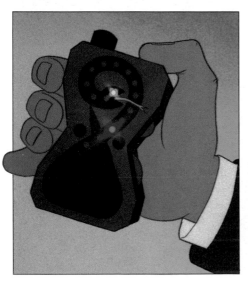

And from behind his snake-shaped desk, El Supremo took the call, while the evil Messina herself coiled around his shoulder. "Yesssss?" he hissed, menacingly.

"We have failed," wailed the spy leader.

"*Failed*?" shouted El Supremo.

"Yes," cringed the leader. "We have failed to kill FR07."

"Fools! Imbeciles!" spat El Supremo.

"You were under instructions to follow and observe – not to kill! Return at once to your section, and prepare for tonight's attack."

"The target for tonight is Big Ben! Big Ben, do you hear me? Big Ben!" bellowed El Supremo.

And Freddie looked very thoughtful. "Big Ben? *Voilà!*"

Back at the race track, Number Seven had just won the race, and Daffers and Scotty were jumping up and down with pleasure.

"Good old Number Seven!" cried Daffers. Scotty was delighted too.

"How did you know it
would win, Freddie?"
asked Daffers admiringly.
   "Well," replied Freddie
with a smile, "it's my
lucky number – and I got
it straight from the
horse's mouth!"

"In fact," Freddie continued,
"I know a lot of things, my
dear Daffers. For instance, I
know where the enemy are
going to attack next!"
   "Well?" replied Daffers.
"What's the target? We must
tell the Brigadier immediately."

"Ah yes, you will,
won't you?" murmured
Freddie. "Very well.
The target is – Windsor
Castle!"

Freddie was up against his old enemy, Messina. She and El Supremo had amassed a huge army of the world's most dastardly criminals in their underground headquarters, which was packed with all the very latest technology and scientific gadgets. And Messina ruled over it all!

Her terrible song hypnotised everyone who was unlucky enough to fall under Messina's power.

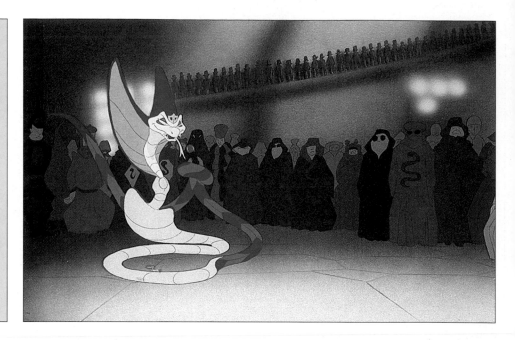

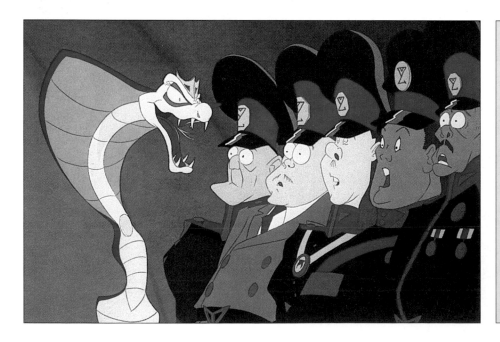

It struck fear into the hearts of all who heard it. Even the fiercest of soldiers found themselves enslaved by her spell.

"Evilmania!
I'm going to rule your world,
Tease you, freeze you,
    squeeze you,
Till you drop!
I can hypnotise,
Hit you right between
    the eyes . . ."

The army marched to the rhythm of Messina's song.

"My poison bites -
Puts out the lights -
And then you stop!
Yes, I'm the Queen!
Yes, I'm the Queen!
The Queen of Evilmania!"

"Are you tired, my beauty?" asked El Supremo, as Messina finished her song, and curled herself around him. "I promise you will soon have your favourite delicacy – frog's legs, with all the trimmings!"

Just then, the video on El Supremo's desk came to life. It was the submarine commander.
  "You'll have the signal tomorrow," said El Supremo.

"You will be able to go ashore with your troops, and conquer the British Isles!"
  "Thank you El Supremo. We're ready – ready and waiting!"

That evening, outside Windsor Castle . . .

. . . the Brigadier was trying his best. "I'm terribly sorry, Your Majesty, but until we get all this sorted out, you'd better go somewhere else!"

The window above the Brigadier slammed shut.

And while the Brigadier winced in despair, Trilby smirked with secret pleasure.

In the meantime, the Frogmobile had taken Freddie, Daffers and Scotty to Big Ben.

The three companions got out of the car, and Nicole sped away.

54

They climbed right up inside Big Ben to the clock room.

"I don't get it," said Scotty. "If the enemy's going to attack Windsor Castle, what are we doing *here*?"

Freddie smiled. "I'm afraid I told a fib," he explained. "*This* is the target."

"It was necessary to distract the Brigadier," he continued. "As a soldier, he would want to capture the enemy."

"But that is not enough! We must penetrate their headquarters. And the only way to do that, is to let *them* take *us*!"

Daffers and Scotty
looked at each
other in dismay.
Then Daffers
took out her
walkie-talkie.

"Brigadier G? Brigadier G?
Are you receiving me?"
But Freddie showed
Daffers the batteries
he'd removed from the
walkie-talkie.

"You waste your time,"
he said calmly.

The Brigadier was still at Windsor Castle, trying to explain the situation to the Queen.

"I was only trying to say that I have a plan, Your Majesty," he panted as her coach sped away.

But just then, over central London, a sinister snake-shaped space ship slithered silently through the sky, towards Big Ben.

A beam of light shot from the head of the ship, and Big Ben began to shake.

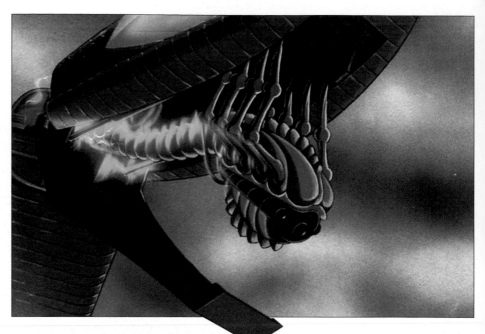

"Going up!" said Freddie quietly. "Hold on tight!"

In a panic, Scotty pulled out a gun from his coat, and pointed it wildly around him.

"Who are you going to shoot, Scotty?" asked Freddie calmly. "Put it away! Enjoy the flight!"

At Windsor, the Brigadier was still expecting the Castle to disappear at any moment.

Then an officer rushed up to him. "Sir! Big Ben – it's gone!"

"Oh no!" groaned the Brigadier. "Alert the fighter planes!"

"I already have, Sir."

"Not here, you idiots!" shouted the Brigadier at the planes. "Go that way! Towards Westminster!"

"Well, so much for Froggie intelligence, eh?" sneered Trilby. The Brigadier was puzzled. "But where *is* Freddie? And Daffers? Daffers, come in, wherever you are!"

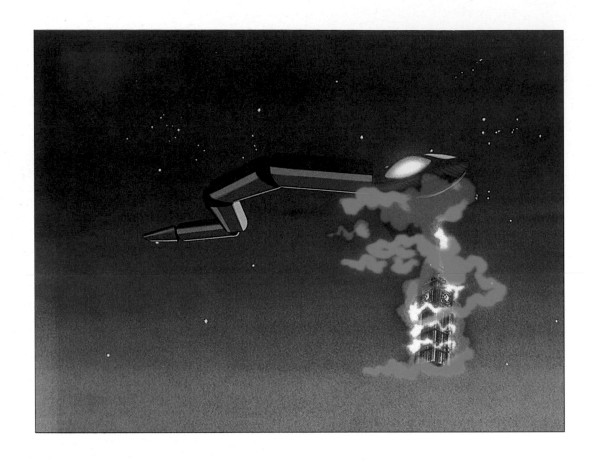

And Big Ben, suspended
beneath the space ship,
was carried swiftly away.

Freddie Goes to London

Secret agent Freddie the Frog is brought in to solve the sinister disappearance of Britain's greatest monuments

THE ADVENTURES OF FREDDIE THE FROG, SECRET AGENT AND AMPHIBIAN EXTRAORDINAIRE, IN ONE STORYBOOK AND FOUR CARTOON BOOKS

WARNER BOOKS

U.K.   £3.99

ISBN 0-356-20115-5

00399

9 780356 201153